How A Princess Survives Hair Day

By Danielle Gordon

Illustrated By Quratulain Iqbal

How a princess survives hair day

Copyright 2019 Danielle Gordon

All rights reserved. Published 2019. Published by Afro Princess Publishing, LLC. This book or any portion thereof may not be reproduced or used in any manner whatsoever without the express written permission of the publisher except for the use of brief quotations in a book review.

For permission please contact afroprincesspub@gmail.com.

ISBN-13:978-0692196724
ISBN-10:0692196722
Afro Princess Publishing, LLC

To all the princesses who had to sit for far too long

I don't like hair day,
It takes way too long.

But, since washing our hair
has to get done,
let's see if we can make hair day
much more fun.

What can a
princess do when
mama washes her hair?

Tell knock-knock jokes to a purple
teddy bear!

What can a princess do while her hair dries?

Paint her nails, write a book, or help make some pies.

How can a princess' mom get rid of those tangles?

With conditioner and fingers,
Careful not to mangle!

What can a princess do when she gets tired of sitting?

Take a break. Do a dance.
Mama too! No kidding!

What can a princess do when she feels the pain?

Say, "Ouch!", to mama. She may relieve the strain.

What can a princess do when the braiding takes too long?

Make up a silly, willy, nilly, dilly song!

How can a princess' mom lay down those edges?

With lots of hair gel and a toothbrush with wedges.

What can a princess do when her hair is done?

Shout hurray, you're through the day, now go have some fun.

What can a princess do when it's time for bed?

Wrap a pretty silk scarf all around her head.

What can a princess do when it's time to pray?

Thank God for coily hair that's special in every way.

THE END

Here are some other fun things you can do on hair day

1- Write in a journal

2- Watch a movie

3- Read a book

4- Write a screenplay

5- Listen to music

6- Color

7- Do a puzzle

8- Paint

9- Cross stitch

10- Knit a blanket

11- Make cookies

12- Ask your mom what she used to do on hair day

13- Bake a cake

14- Take a nap

15- Make jewelry

16- Write someone a letter

17- Do a crossword puzzle

18- Write a song

19- Make a vision board

20- Stretch or do yoga

21- Write a poem

22- Plan a party

23- Look through old family photos

Your turn!
What are some other fun things you can do on hair day?

Make a list below

About the Author

Danielle is Founder and CEO of Afro Princess Publishing, LLC. The company seeks to instill positive self-image in children. She is also the author of 'Whitney's Wonderful Imagination' and 'I'm a Little Superhero' available on Amazon.

Made in the USA
Middletown, DE
25 July 2019